12
FEMINIST

BE KIND
STOP
COOL!

This book is dedicated to every child and adult
who has ever felt different or not good enough.
You can have the life you want and deserve because
you have the tools to attain it. You are perfectly
designed . . . and please never forget that.
—Love, K.B. and J.B.

For my sweet nephew Mikael.
—A.S.

First Published in the USA 2019 by Henry Holt and Company
First published in the UK 2019 by Macmillan Children's Books
This edition published 2020 by Macmillan Children's Books
an imprint of Pan Macmillan
The Smithson, 6 Briset Street, London, EC1M 5NR
Associated companies throughout the world
www.panmacmillan.com

ISBN PB: 978 1 5290 3614 5
ISBN EB: 978 1 5290 3759 3

1 3 5 7 9 8 6 4 2

A CIP catalogue record for this book is available from the British Library.

Printed in China

I Am Perfectly Designed

Karamo Brown and Jason "Rachel" Brown
Illustrated by Anoosha Syed

Macmillan Children's Books

First there was you, Dad.

Then there was me.

And now there is us!

That's right.
Now there is us.

When you first saw me, you said,
“He is perfectly designed, from his head to his toes.”

And I meant every word. Still do.

When I was a baby, I looked just like you . . .

Only I had no hair, and you had lots.

Now . . . it’s the opposite.

So true.

The first thing I remember is being
carried on your shoulders while you walked me all over the city.

Remember that?
I had such a big baby head!

**Indeed.
But your big baby
head was perfectly
designed for you.**

When I was really little, I thought
you could touch the moon. Remember that?
We'd sit on the roof and reach for it.

One day, you'll be big enough to reach it yourself.

But until then, it's perfectly fine to ask for help.

Remember when we
dressed up as syrup and waffles
for Halloween, Dad?

Ha! I do, I do.

That was awesome.
I wonder what
we'll be this year!

When I run in the park,

jump in the park,

climb trees in the park,

and pretend I am a
statue in the park,
you remind me I am perfectly
designed to explore the world.

You are, and you always will be.

ALAD

Sometimes, Dad,
when I get mad,

or sad,

or confused,

you wrap me in your arms.
I like that.

Me, too.
And I remind you that you are
perfectly designed and wonderful.
No matter what you're feeling.

Dad . . . when I grow up and leave home—
will you miss me?

Yes. Very much.

Will you go into my room and play
with my racing cars and cuddly toys?

You know I will!

CHO

Will you sit on the fire
escape and feed the pigeons
like we do in the summer?

The pigeons *and* the sparrows.

Will you
remember our
favourite moves?

**I will, and I'll invent
some new ones, too.**

Dad . . . will you always think of me?

Always.

You know what, Dad?

What?

I will always remember walking through the city
and sitting on your shoulders.
And maybe when you're older, and I'm taller . . .

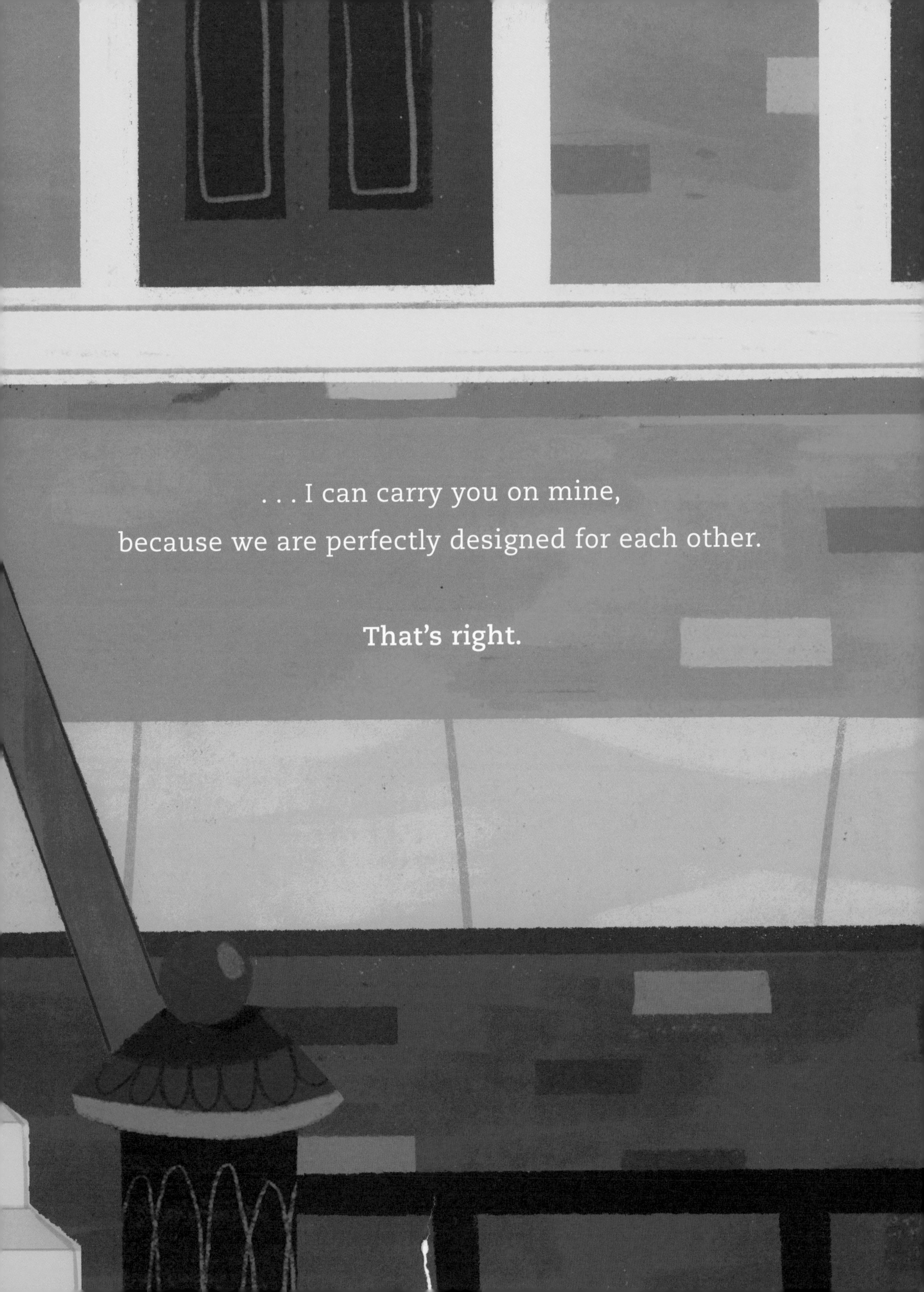

. . . I can carry you on mine,

because we are perfectly designed for each other.

That's right.

Dear Reader,

It's always been a dream of mine to write a story inspired by the many lessons my father has taught me. When I was growing up, anytime I felt fear or uncertainty, my father would remind me that I was perfectly designed.

Knowing that at an early age really instilled self-love and confidence in me, which had been hard to find on my own. Now that I'm older, it's easier to walk with my head held up proudly. My father and I felt it was only right to give this message to you.

We want readers to never forget that just being your natural self is perfect. It's beautiful in every sense. We know how hard it is to think otherwise, but you can't stop telling yourself this until you feel it! Like everything in life, it takes some time. But with repetition, you will learn to walk with your head held higher than the Eiffel Tower.

—Jason Brown

That's exactly right.

—Karamo Brown

12
FEMINIST

BE
KIND
STOP
COOL